Reading Together

The Big Wide-Mouthed Frog

Read it together

This traditional tale about a big wide-mouthed frog is simply told and packs a powerful message about boasting. The humorous illustrations will draw children into the book, as will reading the story aloud. Along with the frog, children will encounter one Australian wild animal after another.

"I'm a possum," said Possum, "and I eat blossom."

"Well, I'm a big wide-mouthed frog!"

Reading aloud is the best way to help your child get to know and enjoy any book, especially a traditional tale. Children will begin to recognize the pattern of the story and the different voices of each character.

It looks like the emu's got four toes!

I think this one is the emu's heel.

Talking together about the story and pictures helps children to understand the book better. Encourage them to ask questions and say what they enjoy about it.

The repeated phrases on each page make it easy for children to remember the story and join in the reading. Gradually they will learn to match the words they say to those they see written down.

Once there was a big wide-mouthed frog...

That says frog.

"Ho there, Upside-down Creature!"

HO THERE!

Each animal has its own personality in this story. By changing your voice to match each one, the story is made more enjoyable and memorable. Children will learn to do this when they come to read for themselves.

I wonder if Frog is going to be quieter from now on?

The surprise ending is one that many children will want to talk about. Perhaps they had a different ending in mind for the story? They can imagine what the frog does next and wonder if he learnt his lesson.

Someone might eat him if he isn't.

For Andrés

First published 1999 by Walker Books Ltd
87 Vauxhall Walk, London SE11 5HJ

This edition published 2007

2 4 6 8 10 9 7 5 3 1

Text © 1999 Walker Books Ltd
Illustrations © 1999 Ana Martín Larrañaga
Introductory and concluding notes © 2001 CLPE/LB Southwark

This book has been typeset in ITC Highlander

Printed in China

British Library Cataloguing in Publication Data:
a catalogue record for this book is available
from the British Library

ISBN 978-1-4063-1416-8

www.walkerbooks.co.uk

The Big Wide-Mouthed Frog

A Traditional Tale

Illustrated by
Ana Martín Larrañaga

WALKER BOOKS
AND SUBSIDIARIES
LONDON · BOSTON · SYDNEY · AUCKLAND

Once there was a big wide-mouthed frog with the biggest, widest mouth you ever did see.

And one day that big
wide-mouthed frog
hopped off to see
the world.

The first creature he met
had big thumping feet.

"Hey, you! Big Thumping Feet!
Who are you and what do you eat?"
shouted the wide-mouthed frog.
"I'm a kangaroo," said Kangaroo,
"and I eat grass."
"Well, I'm a big wide-mouthed frog!"
shouted the wide-mouthed frog.
"And I eat flies!"

The second creature
he met had a big
black nose.

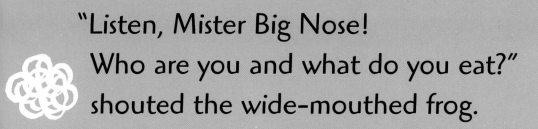

"Listen, Mister Big Nose!
Who are you and what do you eat?"
shouted the wide-mouthed frog.

"I'm a koala," said Koala,
"and I eat leaves."
"Well, I'm a big wide-mouthed frog!"
shouted the wide-mouthed frog.
"And I eat flies!"

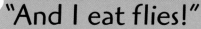

The third
creature
he met was
hanging
upside down.

"Ho there,
Upside-down Creature!
Who are you and what do you eat?"
shouted the wide-mouthed frog.
"I'm a possum," said Possum,
"and I eat blossom."
"Well, I'm a big wide-mouthed frog!"
shouted the wide-mouthed frog.
"And I eat flies!"

The fourth creature he met
had three long toes.
"Look here, Three Long Toes!
Who are you and what do you eat?"
shouted the wide-mouthed frog.

"I'm an emu," said Emu,
"and I eat grasshoppers."
"Well, I'm a big wide-mouthed frog!"
shouted the wide-mouthed frog.
"And I eat flies!"

Then the wide-mouthed frog
met a creature stretched out
on the riverbank like a
knobbly brown log.

"HEY, Knobbly Brown Log!
Who are you and what do
you eat?" shouted the
wide-mouthed frog.

Knobbly Brown Log opened her mouth in a slow, wide, lazy smile.

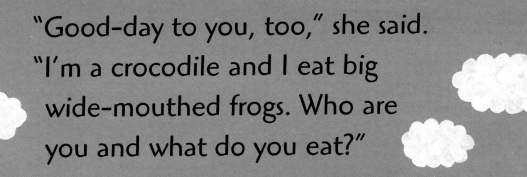

"Good-day to you, too," she said. "I'm a crocodile and I eat big wide-mouthed frogs. Who are you and what do you eat?"

"Me?" whispered the wide-mouthed frog, puckering his mouth into the smallest, narrowest mouth you ever did see.

I'm

off!"

Read it again

Tell the story

Encourage your child to tell the story in their own words, using the pictures to help them. As they get to know it well, they will begin to use more words and phrases from the book.

Speech balloons

Each animal has a lot to say, especially the wide-mouthed frog. Write down what each animal says about itself as a speech balloon and match it to the picture.

Zigzag book

With help, children can make up their own story about a wide-mouthed frog who meets five more animals. They might like to use the same pattern as the story. Together you can then make a zigzag book, with your child drawing as you write.

What am I?

Play the animal guessing game. Take it in turns to describe an animal for the other person to guess. You can start with animals in the book, then try others.

I am cuddly and I have a shiny black nose. Who am I?

A bear? Koala!

That knobbly log looks like a crocodile to me.

I have big sharp teeth and I eat frogs!

Acting out

This is a good story to act out because of the strong pattern and animal characters. Children can be the different animals including the "knobbly brown log".

Yes, and can you find where the dog card goes?

My name has a "d".

Animal ABC game

Write the alphabet on a long strip of paper. Encourage your child to draw pictures of animals for each letter and label them. Then help them to match the animals to the letters on the strip.